History

P9-EDF-683

# OREGON TRAIL, 1843

## OREGON COUNTRY
(disputed by United States and Britain)

Rocky Mountains

Crow

Continental Divide

Crossing into Oregon Country

SOUTH PASS

FORT BRIDGER

Wind River Mountains

Green River Valley

Bear River

Grand Teton Mountains

Shoshone

SODA SPRINGS

Nez Perce

FORT HALL

Cayuse

Umatilla

Flagstaff Hill

Bannock

Our settlers traveled on the Snake River north side of the Snake River for a while, then crossed back.

FORT BOISE

The Great Salt Lake

Snake River

said good-bye to 20 families

Walla Walla

Blue Mountains

Emigrant Hill

Idaho Mountains

California Trail

Wasco

THE DALLES

Paiute

MEXICO

Chinook

Klamath

Shoshone

Columbia River

OREGON CITY

N
E
S
W

Willamette River Valley

# UNITED STATES TERRITORIES

Great Plains

Ute

Rocky Mountains

Continental Divide

INDEPENDENCE ROCK

Sweetwater River

Just about halfway there!

wrote our names

Arapaho

Northern Cheyenne

FORT LARAMIE

met Indians

CHIMNEY ROCK

SCOTT'S BLUFF

COURT-HOUSE ROCK

saw buffalo

tough river crossing

Southern Cheyenne

Arapaho

Lakota Sioux

Platte River

Oto

Kansa

Pawnee

Kickapoo
Potawatomi

Missouri River

Great Plains

The Oregon Trail

UNITED STATES

INDEPENDENCE, MISSOURI

The locations of many Native American tribes are noted on this map. That doesn't mean the tribes always stayed in one area, though. They moved from place to place, so that it was not unusual for the wagon train to meet Crow in a region mostly populated by Cheyenne.

CANADA

OREGON COUNTRY

LOUISIANA PURCHASE

MEXICO

REPUBLIC OF TEXAS

UNITED STATES OF AMERICA

To Joyanne Bates, Master Teacher and Travelin' Gal

–D.S.

To my fellow trailmates Chris, Izzy and Gwen and the Bentonite Cowboy

–H.B.

Roughing It on the Oregon Trail Text copyright © 2000 by Diane Stanley Illustrations copyright © 2000 by Holly Berry Printed in Singapore. Library of Congress Cataloging-in-Publication Data Stanley, Diane. Roughing it on the Oregon Trail / by Diane Stanley ; illustrated by Holly Berry. p. cm. "Joanna Cotler Books." Summary: Twins Liz and Lenny, along with their time-traveling grandmother, join a group of pioneers journeying west on the Oregon Trail in 1843. ISBN 0-06-027065-9 — ISBN 0-06-027066-7 (lib. bdg.) — ISBN 0-06-449006-8 (pbk.) 1. Oregon Trail—Juvenile fiction. [1. Oregon Trail—Fiction. 2. Overland journeys to the Pacific—Fiction. 3. Frontier and pioneer life—West (U.S.)—Fiction. 4. Time travel—Fiction.] I. Berry, Holly, ill. II. Title. III. Series: Stanley, Diane. Time-traveling twins. PZ7.S7869Ro 2000 98-41711 [Fic]–dc21 CIP AC Typography by Alicia Mikles ❖ Visit us on the World Wide Web! www.harperchildrens.com

◆ THE TIME-TRAVELING TWINS ◆

# Roughing It *on the* Oregon Trail

by DIANE STANLEY

Illustrated by HOLLY BERRY

JOANNA COTLER BOOKS

An Imprint of HarperCollinsPublishers

Our parents were going on a two-week trip to Paris, where you have to sit politely through long meals and be very well behaved in the hotel.
That was why we went to stay with Grandma.
Now, she's not like any other grandmother we know.
She's always studying up on our ancestors, and her walls are covered with portraits of people who lived long, long ago.
As if this weren't weird enough, imagine our surprise when, right after our parents left, Grandma asked us which one of our ancestors we'd like to visit!

We decided to visit our great-great-great-grandmother Elizabeth. But first we had to change our clothes. Grandma said we couldn't go out west in 1843 wearing shorts and T-shirts.

Wow! This dress looks like it was made by hand.

I'll just go as I am.

When we were finally ready, Grandma put on her magic hat. Then we all held hands and closed our eyes and waited. Suddenly we felt very strange. . . .

When we opened our eyes, things had really changed.

Pretty soon we found the wagon we were looking for.
Walking beside it was our great-great-great-grandmother Elizabeth.
Of course, in 1843, she was only ten years old.
Grandma told Elizabeth's family that we were distant relatives and we didn't have a wagon.
They said we could ride with them.

Usually we walked.
If we got really tired, though,
we rode in the wagon.
It was crowded and very bumpy.
You couldn't see much.

Yow!
This thing needs
shock absorbers!

It is pretty rough. But that's not
surprising, since there isn't really
any road here—just a few wagon
ruts. And, of course, the wheels
have iron "tires"! But you might as
well get used to it, dear, because
it's going to get a whole lot worse.

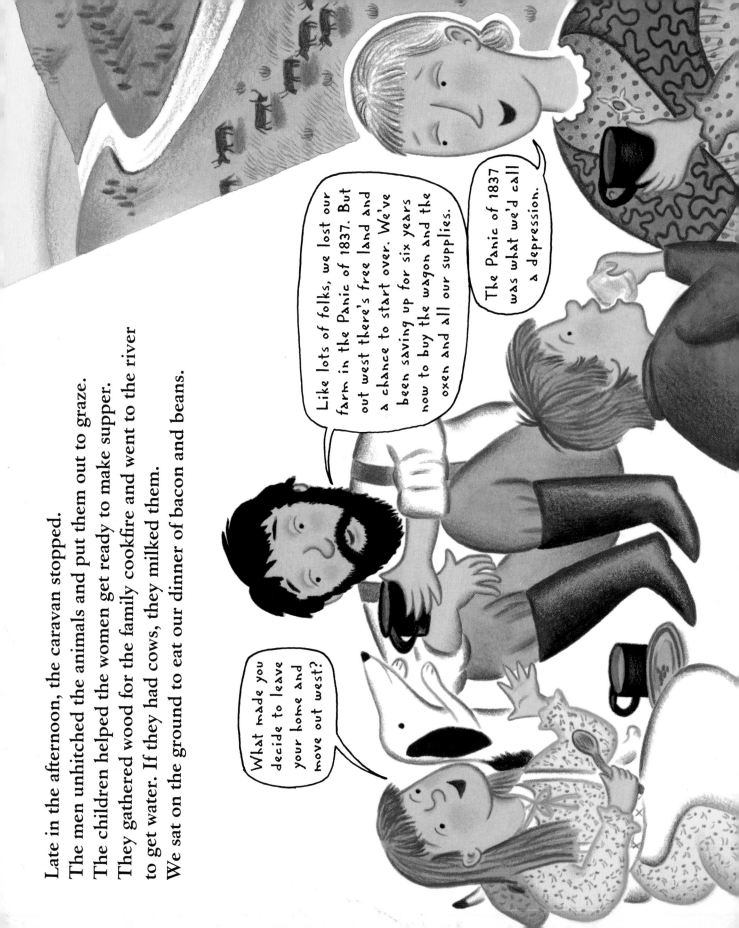

Late in the afternoon, the caravan stopped.
The men unhitched the animals and put them out to graze.
The children helped the women get ready to make supper.
They gathered wood for the family cookfire and went to the river
to get water. If they had cows, they milked them.
We sat on the ground to eat our dinner of bacon and beans.

Like lots of folks, we lost our farm in the Panic of 1837. But out west there's free land and a chance to start over. We've been saving up for six years now to buy the wagon and the oxen and all our supplies.

The Panic of 1837 was what we'd call a depression.

What made you decide to leave your home and move out west?

Later, while we were scouring the pots and washing the dishes, Elizabeth's mother mixed some dried beans with water and a little bacon. Then she dug a hole, filled it with hot coals, and put the bean pot in it. The beans would cook slowly overnight, she said. All she'd have to do the next day was heat them up for dinner.

Want to go bark at the cattle?

Pretty soon, someone began playing his fiddle, and he was joined by a fellow with a harmonica, or "mouth organ," as they called it. We danced and sang and had a great time.

Turkey in the Straw, Haw, haw, haw . . .

Hey, I know that one!

I hear it's a real paradise for raising cattle out there. A man just has to turn 'em out to pasture and wait to get rich.

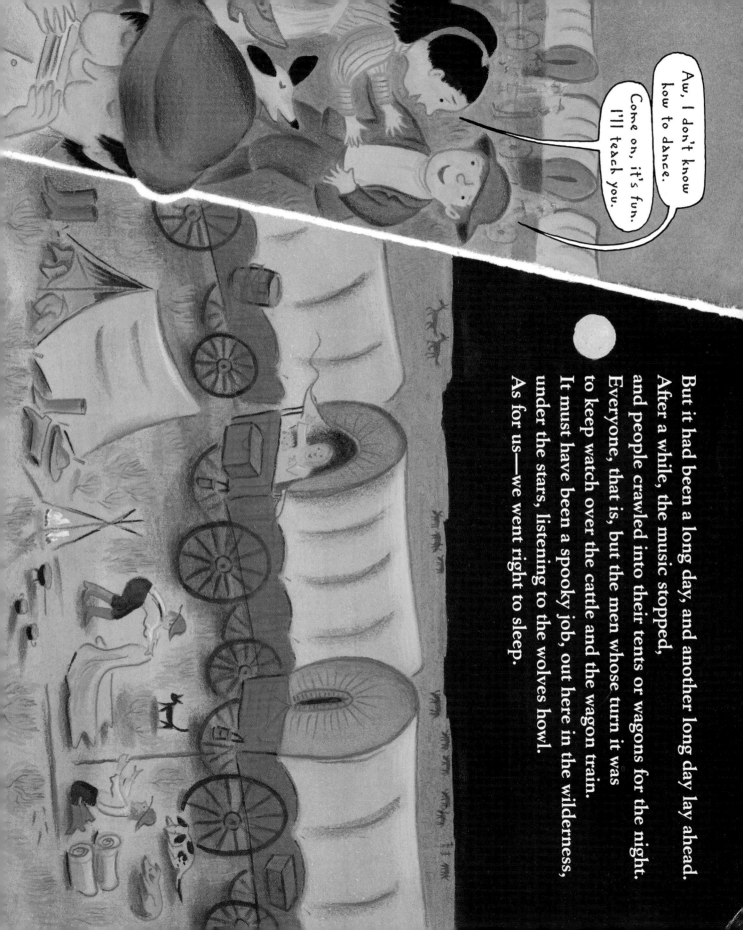

But it had been a long day, and another long day lay ahead.
After a while, the music stopped,
and people crawled into their tents or wagons for the night.
Everyone, that is, but the men whose turn it was
to keep watch over the cattle and the wagon train.
It must have been a spooky job, out here in the wilderness,
under the stars, listening to the wolves howl.
As for us—we went right to sleep.

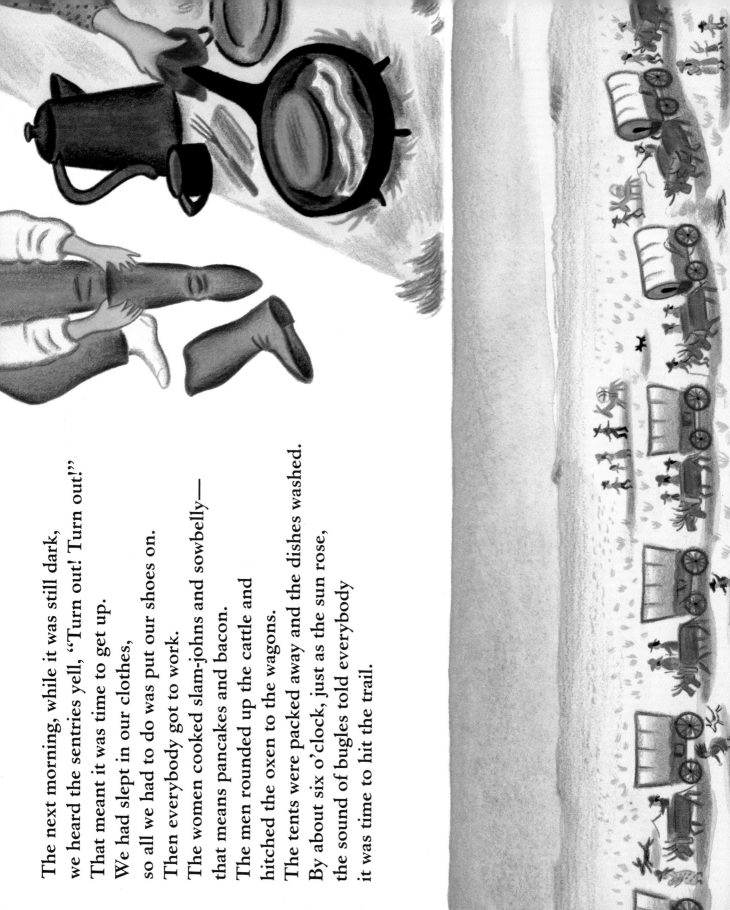

The next morning, while it was still dark,
we heard the sentries yell, "Turn out! Turn out!"
That meant it was time to get up.
We had slept in our clothes,
so all we had to do was put our shoes on.
Then everybody got to work.
The women cooked slam-johns and sowbelly—
that means pancakes and bacon.
The men rounded up the cattle and
hitched the oxen to the wagons.
The tents were packed away and the dishes washed.
By about six o'clock, just as the sun rose,
the sound of bugles told everybody
it was time to hit the trail.

Life on the Oregon Trail was pretty much the same, day after day: hot and very, very dusty. Because of all the dust, everybody wanted their wagon to be up front. To be fair to all the families, whoever got to be in front one day went to the rear the next. That way, nobody argued about it. Soon we came to a wide, muddy river called the Platte and followed it, going west.

Then one great day we saw our first herd of buffalo.
We could see them off in the distance, raising a great cloud of dust.
You could feel the ground tremble as they passed.
Men grabbed their guns and powder horns and rode off after them.
It meant we would have fresh meat.
I don't think anybody dreamed that in a few years
there would hardly be any buffalo left.

Sometimes we had to cross rivers.
If there was a shallow section, we just drove across.
After all, the wagons were pretty high.
But some rivers were too deep to ford,
so we wrapped the wagons in buffalo hides
and coated them with tallow and ashes.
This made them waterproof.
We took the wheels off the wagons and
floated them across like boats. The animals had to swim.
You needed to be careful with the mules, though.
If they got water in their ears, they might go into a panic and drown.
But all our animals made it just fine.

After a while the trail got rougher.

It was hot, and we were tortured by sand flies and mosquitoes.

The animals suffered too, grunting and flicking their tails to drive them away.

The trail began to slope upward, toward the mountains.

We passed landmarks such as Courthouse Rock and Chimney Rock, named by the trappers who passed there in the 1820s.

We were just past Scott's Bluff when word was passed down the line of wagons that the pilot had seen signs of Indians.

Sure. The Indians take the hides off the lodge poles, pack everything on their ponies, and head off for a better hunting spot. They even use the lodge poles to help carry things. They attach a pole on either side of a horse or dog and put a buffalo-hide platform between them, called a travois. The poles drag along the ground. Those are the marks the pilot saw.

A village? Can a village go from place to place?

Pilot says he saw marks of lodge poles in the sand. He thinks an Indian village passed by here in the last day or so.

Dogs as beasts of burden? Don't get any ideas!

We stopped by a spring at midday.
For "nooning," we never took the time to make fires and cook.
We ate cold beans and biscuits while the animals grazed and rested.
All at once everyone stopped talking—Indians were approaching.
We watched as they rode peacefully into our camp, then got down
from their horses. The leader asked to see our "chief," so the pilot
came forward and they shook hands. The Indian who spoke was a
Crow chief named Yellow Feather. He sat down in a circle with
our pilot and some other men and took out his red clay pipe.
They mixed tobacco with red willow bark, and took turns smoking it.
The pilot offered them some dried buffalo meat.
After a while they shook hands again, and the Indians went away.

Finally we reached Fort Laramie and set up camp nearby.
It wasn't a military fort—the nearest soldiers were back in the United States,
seven hundred miles to the east.
Fort Laramie was a trading center, where we could buy supplies,
repair wagons, get horses shod, and rest.
We had been gone forty days and still had a long way to go.

When we headed back out on the trail, things got even harder. The wind swept endlessly across the prairie, and the nights were cold. There was hardly even any sagebrush for our cookfires. We had to burn buffalo chips instead.

Hey, guess what Jed shot—an antelope! Fresh meat for dinner!

Come on, Liz. If we don't hurry, all the buffalo chips will be taken.

Buffalo chips? Is that what I think it is? Are we really supposed to pick it up? Are we truly going to cook our food over . . .

I think the word you're looking for is "dung."

We stopped at a place called Independence Rock.
People called it the "register" of the Oregon Trail.
We mixed grease and gunpowder to make paint and
wrote our names on the rock beside all the other names
of people who had been there before us.

The trail got even rougher as we climbed the rocky slope of the Wind River Mountains.
At last we reached the top at South Pass, and crossed the Continental Divide.
That's the point where all the rivers start to flow west instead of east.
Then the trail led us back down the slope and into Oregon country.
We stopped for the night in the beautiful Green River valley.
It had once been full of beaver, but even in 1843 there are scarcely any left.
They had been caught by trappers and turned into gentlemen's top hats.

Before heading up into the Grand Teton mountains,
we rested in the lush meadows near the Bear River.
We ate fresh trout and elk with wild onions.
There were even berries for dessert.
Later we stopped at Soda Springs,

Let's gather as many of these wild onions and berries as we can. We'll be glad to have them later.

I thought you hated fish.

That was when I could afford to be picky.

where the water came out all bubbly
and tickled your nose when you drank it.
At Fort Hall we said good-bye to about twenty families.
They turned off to the southwest,
following the California Trail to San Francisco.

We all had to get out and walk, up to our ankles in mud. Everybody was so tired and hungry by the time we reached the mountains that some were near despair.

As we went higher, it grew cold and began to snow, even though it was only September.
The slopes on the other side were so steep, we had to ease the wagons down on ropes anchored to trees. But by then, lots of people didn't have wagons anymore.

At last we reached the Columbia River.
From there you could travel by raft
to the lush Willamette River valley.
Though that would be the end of the journey,
starting a new life wouldn't be easy for Elizabeth's family.
They had to cut down trees to build a cabin before winter,
and they needed to clear fields of rocks and brush
for planting crops in the spring.
It was the end of the trail for us, too—time to go home.
We hated to say good-bye,
knowing we'd never see them again.

We made it—and what beautiful country! I just know we'll build a good life here!

I'll miss you so much!

Sniff!

Boy, we sure had some adventures together!

When the last boat was out of sight,
we stood there on the riverbank for a while.
Then Grandma put on her hat, and we all
held hands and closed our eyes and waited.
Everything happened just like before,
and we were back at Grandma's.

Grandma, what
happened to them all?

Well, Jed took over the farm after his father died. He married that red-haired girl named Cora—remember her?—and they had three children. Martha grew up to be a teacher, helping a whole generation of young Americans learn to read and write in a little one-room schoolhouse. As for Elizabeth, she eventually married a kindhearted rancher named James who came down the Oregon Trail in the summer of 1844, and they had six children. Their third daughter, Sofia, was my great-grandmother.

I'm so glad it all turned out OK.

I remember Cora. She had the little spotted dog with the beautiful eyes.

When Mom and Dad came to pick us up, they told us all about their trip to Paris. They said it had been a great adventure. We thought that was pretty funny! But we just winked at Grandma and didn't say a word. We know how to keep a secret.

When it was time to leave, Grandma handed us each a present.

POETRY
by

Dear Liz and Lenny,
 This is so you will
always remember
Elizabeth and Jed and
 Martha—and their great
trek on the Oregon Trail.
 And now, my little
 pioneers—where shall
 we go next?      Love,
                Grandma

# AUTHOR'S NOTE

The story of Liz and Lenny along the Oregon Trail shows only one small part of a very big picture, an epic clash of two very different cultures. The European settlers who came to the Americas firmly believed that any land that was not formally parceled off as belonging to some state or individual—with a legal document to prove it—was up for grabs. So grab they did. Many different nations—including Britain, France, Spain, Mexico, Russia, and the United States—claimed to "own" certain parts of the land on the American continent. The Native American peoples, who had been living there all along, were particularly vulnerable to this land grab because their many nations were not united, nor as well armed, and because they didn't believe in "owning" land—they thought it belonged to the earth and all who lived on it.

It is all history now, complete with its rights and wrongs. The best we can do is try to understand what happened and why.

—D.S.

The Oregon Trail stretches 2,170 miles from the Missouri River to the Willamette River, and was traveled by over 400,000 settlers between 1840 and 1880. Three hundred miles of trails are still discernible today, and an auto route can be followed from Independence, Missouri, to Oregon City, Oregon.

For more information about the trail, contact:
Oregon National Historic Trail ✳ National Park Service
Long Distance Trails Office ✳ 324 South State Street ✳ Suite 250
P.O. Box 45155 ✳ Salt Lake City, UT 84145-0155